MENTAL

RAW VERSION

YOGENDRA NIKALE

mental phone calls customer care.
mental watches a guy pushing a bike with his leg on th road. and
menatl starts doing the same to everyone.

written by : yogendra nikale.
tittle : mental
in a school a lecture was going on, students were of 8 years old.
teacher was explaining the children by writting on the black board.
every child in the classroom were listening to the teacher, except
mathew.
mathew was laughing nonstop watching teachers face.
teacher notices mathew.
teacher yells at mathew : mathew, whats so funny, why are you
laughing.
mathew stops laughing
teacher : get up mathew. tell us what joke you have. let the entire
class laugh.
mathew gets up and says" nothing teacher, its nothing"
teacher : you know fools laugh with no reason, sit down now and
concenterate. ok where was i [and starts taeching again]
mathew sits down
the teacher starts teaching again.
and starts laughing again watchin teacher's face.
teacher's face close up shot.
mathew laughing close up shot.
teacher notices mathew. and yells mathew.
cut to
mother of mathew wipping him and talking to him.
mathew : mama, i was just laughing. it was funny. watching her talk
for no reason. i didnt do anything wrong.
mother : i know my child, my father was same like you, should i tell

you one thing. one day when you grow up. you can laugh, sing and do what ever you like.

cut to

in a fun fair at night everyone were enjoying their rides.

mathew is all grown up and now he is working in the fun fair

mathew and his co workers were getting instructions from the boss.

boss : last night the you made ride too long. keep it short. so they can rebuy the ticket and go for the second one. alright everyone just move. fast get back to your stations and starts working your ass up.

all the workers starts moving and the boss stops mathew.

boss : listen you nut case. you are good for nothing. you go out and just manage the cue.

mathew : but im the counter guy.

boss : fell lucky you got this job. or you will be picking garbage from the street when the night is over. now get the fuck out here.

mathew comes out and starts managig the crowd.

mathew watches the boss having a cigar and watching every ride.

mathew getting phych watching him. and music playing in his head.

mathew watches the guy comes out from IT room and waves at boss and boss also waves back.

mathew watching it starts walking towards the room in anger.

IT room is a room where the technical part of all the rides.

mathew watches the buttons and start playing with it.

the light of the fun fair starts flickering.

the boss notices and says "what the fuck is this"

mathew then starts pulling the pluggiins.

the ride starts going reverse all of them.

mathew then speeeds up the ride.

boss watching the speed of the ride looks at the IT room.

mathew then pulls the lever of time and puts its up to 15 mins. in speed and breaks the lever so no one can pull down.

boss comes there and says"what the fuck have you done"
mathew watches him in anger.
boss tries to pull down the lever but he cant. boss gets panicked in
this situation.
mathew comes out and watches.
the rides are going backswards and veryfast and people are puking on
each other.
and boss comes out and watches theis whole disaster.
mathew watches the boss and then the peoplestuck in rides and
smiles
cut to
tittle
cut to
mathew laughing in the police station alone and everyone are
watching him. police and the boss.
mathew remembering the incident and laughing.
boss : who the fuck is this guy.
officer : its a mental case.
boss : how do you know.
officer : because you are not the only one who got fucked by him. well
we got to set him free.
boss : my life is ruined, my reputation is gone. my business is
colapsed. and are letting him go. just like that.
officer : yeah, we cannot take any action againsta a mental case. only
we can set him hospital. if you press charges on him. but the court
and everything. your time and money will be wasted. did you see the
file when came to you for job.
boss watches him laugh and says "let the demon set free then, his
time will come"
cut to
mathew is in a interview for the job of dish anttena t.v.

sir this my file.
the interviewer : what will i do with your expericeince. you just have to fix the dish on the customers house. i dont need any resume for this.
just tell me your name.
[the interviewer writes down his name]
interviewer : now just get started, wear the uniform and start the job.
mathew : now.
interviewer : offcourse now. theres the phone, you will get the call on it. atten it and if required take a guy with you for fixing new connection.
cut to
mathew siiting on desk of phone. waiting for the phone and no one calls and he romes around the office and still no one calls.
plays with the stuff from the desk.
and one guy calls mathew picks up.
customer : hello, is this the dish tv office.
mathew : yes.
customer : the chanels are not working. i think its the network problem.
mathew : well hold on a second
mathew comes out asks the field guy.
the field guy replies "ask him to turn his antena the dish will work"
mathew goes back and speaks on the phone.
the field guy laughs from behind.
the customer comes in the office with the complaint.
customer : what kind of people you have hired. is this the way to talk to the customers.
interviewer : what happened.
customer : i called for a complaint, and your guy replied that turn the dish antena. it will work. is this services you provide.
interviewer to the field guy : who answered the phone.

the field guy : it was not me sir. its the new guy.
interviewer calls mathew. and asks "did you tell him to turn the dish.
mathew : yeas sir. i said so.
interviewer : what the fuck is wrong with you.
mathew : the field guy told me to say so.
field guy : he is lying sir. i would never do such a thing.
mathew : he is lying.
field guy : no, sir i beeen working here for so much time. i old never
do so.
mathew : no sir believe me.
interviewer : i had enough of you.
interviewer to the customer : dont worry sir it will be done right now.
interviewer to field guy : immiedeatly go there and fix his network fast
as possible.
field guy : yes siir. [the customer and the field guy goes together]
interviewer to mathew : have you gone nuts, this s your first day of
job and you are spoiing realtionship with our customers
mathew : no sir.
interviewer : what do you mean by no, this is a last warning, one more
complaint against you. you will be out of here.
cut to
mathew sitting in his cabin and getting restless. walking the entire
office.
the field guy comes after repair, and watching him mathew getting
angry.
starts walking in the entire offfice watching him.
there comes a phone and he answers. "yes this the dish tv office. ok
new connection. can you give me your address.
mathew writes it down and says "we will be there any moment"
cut to
mathew and the field guy are on the road on his bike. and the dish is

tied on the bike.
they stop at the gate of the society.
the watchman doesnt allow them to go inside. he says outside bike is not allowed.
the field guy says you wait here i will park the bike down the road and then we will go together. and gives him his helmet.
mathew takes the helmet and wears it. and gets inside.
there was a guy on the balcony on the phone
mathew shoults are you the guy who called for the dish connection.
the guy from the balcony replies "no , im not the guy"
mathew : who the fuck do you think you are. you didnt even inform the watchman we were coming.
the guy : who are you, and why are you yelling at me. i didnt even call for the tv connection.
mathew : shut the fuck up, it mmust be your wife.
the guy : isten budy. hold your horses. im not married.
mathew : then it must be your mother. who wanted antena on her ass.
the guy : hey, you bastard. what did you say huh.
mathew : wait let me park my bike and come, you are a dead man. you understand.
mathew goes back to the bike and take the dish saying "give me the dish sir, it might be heavy.
and the field guy takes the helmet. and says thank you.
they both enter the gate. the guy from the balcony is in the building compound with men.
the guy asks who was here before and went to park his bike.
the field guy replies "it was me sir"
the building guy starts beating him and mathew watches him smillingly.
cut to

mathew in his house laughing loudly and watching the posters on the
wall. and remembering the field guy getting beaten up.
cut to
mathew on a bike of pizza delivery. delivering food everywhere. shots.
a happy life shots.
in evening mathew gets an order to deliver food and he starts ridding
. a guy on a bike horns him. mathew watches back. the guy is still
horning on him.
mathew gets irritated by his horns several times.
mathew stops at side and lets him pass.
mathew starts following him honking.
the guy gets fed up he stops and mathew also stops aside.
as the guy starts his bike and goes. mathew also follows him honking.
this happens several times.
mathew does this till he gets in his house. mathew watches where he
stays.
cut to
next day that guy comes out of his appartment. and mathew starts
following him honking.
the guy stops in between and joins his hands but still mathew
continues doing it.
the guy reaches his office and watches from his window. mathew is
stilll waiting outside and looking him up from down.
the guy works the whole day time lapse of the watch.
the guy looks from his window mathew is not there. he comes out of
his office and gets on the road again mathew follows him in the
street in evening.
the guy gets fed up and stops the bike. and starts throwing stones on
mathew and the stone a car mirror and the car guy and the bike gets
into a fight.
cut to

mathew goes back to the pizza place and boss says. where were you
you disapeared yesterday. everything ok.
mathew : sir, i had some problem.
boss : what happened, where were you.
mathew : me, i was [starts laughing remembering the entire scene in
front of his eyes]
and everyone from the pizza place stares at him.
cut to
mathew working as a driver. the things were happy.
mathew driving and the owner going to office shots.
mathew waitng for him in the car.
owner of car with family in the car shots.
mathew dropping children to school shots.
owner with girlfriend shots.
mathew asking for payment.
the owner replies " listen you will get next week, my hands are full
tight, now just hit the road i do have long night. "
mathew starts driving. and the owner picks his girl and he gives him a
gift.
girl : wow, it looks real diamond. it must be very expensive.
owner : nah, nothing ies expensive then you.
mathew watching them from the mirror.
cut to
the owner and girl dancing in the disco. and mathew waiting in the
car thinking.
the owner drinking shots and food shots. mathew still waiting in the
car.
cut to
the owner comes down drunk and they both sit in the car.
the car owner says take us to her house.
mathew : ok sir.

mathew starts the car drives in speed.
the owner says : what the fuck are you doing. take it slow.
mathew drives in a very low speed of 10 and all the cars from behind
starts honking.
owner : what the fuck is wrong with you. speed up a bit.
mathew : tell me what you want to do do, speed up or drive slow.
stay on your words.
the owner "ok speed up"
mathew speeds up a lot and drifts takes risky turns.
the ownner tries to open the car window.
but its locked.
owner : "i know what this is about, i didnt do the payment is it."
the girl : how much is his payment i'll give him {she opens her purse]
mathew : its never about payment, its about how you treat me.
mathew starts driving zig zag.
the girl womets in the car. the owner is filled up with vomet and he
also vomet.
mathew drives in speed and dashes a cement truck and the cement
falls all over the car.
mathew comes out of the car and throws his cap on the car and
walks away.
cut to
mathew working in the hotel as waiter. shots.
everything calm. getting his payment properly.
mathew serving people. everything was happy shots.
mathew humble with everyone shots.
mathew throwing garbage shots.
one day mathew was getting ready in the changing room removed his
uniform and kept on the table and he goes In the wash room for a
piss.
and on the table there was a worker smoking and was watching

videos on the phone.
the smoker keeps the smoke on the table and the smoke slides and
burns down the mathews pant when mathew was in the toilet.
the smoker stops the smoke and keeps his pants as it iwas. and there
was a burned hole on the backside of mathews pant.
mathew comes there and weras his pants.
mathew noticees many customers laughs on him watching his back.
he smiles back
time passes and the owner notices his panst are burned from the
back.
the owner tells him change your pants there is hole. he watches it
and everyone laughs on him.
mathew rushes towards the changing room.
cut to
mathew in his casual clothes and watching his burned pants. and the
shift gets over and everyone gathers and laughs on him.
mathew gets angry and when everyone is gone.
mathew takes the whiskey bottle and burns down everyones lockers.
cut to
the hotel gets fired up.
and ambulance comes and stops the fire.
cut to
all the wiaters in the police station.
officer : who burned the hotel.
everyone : no sir i left early. it maybe some accident. we had nothing
to do with the fire. maybe you ask mathew he left late.
mathew is quite.
officer : ok you write all your exit time and you can go. and mr.
mathew you come inside.
everyone starts signing and they go.
officer takes mathew inside.

officer : listen mental, i know you did this. but im letting you go because of your condition. but one more complaint i will put you in assylum my self. because burning down the place is a serious crime, peopple were lucky no one was inside. so be carefull. its your last chance

cut to

mathew enters a shop of a decorators.
mathew doing the lighting. work with people and.
the owner says turn on the switch mathew turns the switch on the lighting works but the entire areas light gets fused and the owner watches it and says ohhh my god and turns back to mathew and mathew says isnt it beautifull.

cut to

mathew in a mall working as train driver and dashes every person on the floor.

cut to

mathew as bunny in a birthday party. a child hits him and he hits him back.

cut to

mathew in elctronic shop.
customer asking what is free with the laptop.
mathew says a pendrive.
customer : and if i take only pendrive.
mathew : then you wiill get the laptop free.
a long queue fighting on the counter.
the counter guy : who told you this.
customer points at mathew.

cut to

mathew runs from the electronic shop and the owner comes running and abbusing.

cut to

mathew as plumber. fixing nut bolts with the plumber partner.
cut to
mathew shows the owner of the house his shower annd the shower
comes from down . and entire pipeline is leaking in the house.
cut to
mathew doing pest control. he puts the pest control in the kitchen
utensils. drinking water and also in refrigerator.
cut to
mathew as painter, painting.
and the entire house isa disaster.
mathew painted even the sofa, photos on the wall and statues also.
and even the gajets were painted.
cut to
mathew working with the undertaker, cleaning the deadbody.
and in funeral when the relatives open the coffin the dead body is in
joker costume
cut to
mathew working as a pan repair. he fixes the fan on the wall.
cut to
naked posters on the children room.
and their mother clossing the children eyes.
cut to
mathew working in a barber shop as a sweeper.
as he was sweeping the oowner troubling him
mathew puts hair removal cream in the face pack tin .
and the the guy who was doing facial his entire face hair gets
removed.
and fight between the owner and the customer and mathew laughing.
cut to
mathew painting the street lines and he make the street lines all
confusiing.

cut to

mathew interview as care taker.

owner : look i only want someone to take care of flat. the flat is empty. you live there cook, you live there. just keep the house clean. there is gy in the society also. but if i hear any complaint you will be fired.

mathew nods his head.

cut to

mathew entering the house. cleaning the house shots. removing cloth from the sofa and everything. living there lavish life.

one day outside his window, he watches a guy showing his muscles aand the girl cheering.

mathew to himself : alright lets go go gym then

cut to

mathew going to gym. and working out.

watching his muscle in the mirror.

cut to

mathew in gym and the owner of the gym treats every one bad. mathew watches it and one guy says what can we do he is the owner of the gym.

and the owner : is everyone out. yes.

mathew watches he is closing the gym.

cut to

mathew watching his body in the mirror.

cut to

taking steam in the steam room.

cut to

eating protien.

cut to

checking his muscle size.

cut to

one day when mathew was working out and the owner comes there and hits on his head. hey get the fuck out of here. and takes mathew's place.

mathew gets angry.

mathew watches him working out all the time in anger.

mathew knows he closes the gym.

cut to

the owner in the steam room and watches mathew is there.

suddenly the owner gets some bad smell.

the owner watches him mathew was shitting.

owner : what the fuck are you doing.

mathew gets up and closes the steam room and the locker room too.

the owner banging. and he doesnt opens the door.

mathew locks the gym too and goes away.

cut to

mathew in his house visualizing how he must have been in the steam room of sheat.

mathew laughing at home. mathew gets a call of his cousin.

mathew picks up : what the fuck do you want.

cousin : hey mathew. its your cousin. how are you.

mathew : im fine, what do you want.

cousin : what are you doing.

mathew looks at the laughing pictures and says "me, m doing nothing"

cousin : hey i will be in the town tomorrow, i have an interview.

mathew : so what the fuck do you want from me.

cousin : i have no place there, can i come there for a day.

mathew : why dont you stay in hotel.

cousin : the hotels are too expensive. come on im your cousin. for one day and also its my birthday.

mathew : alright only 1 day.

cut to

cousin knocks the door. mathew opens.

cousin : hey mathew, hows you man. this place stil looks the same.

mathew : you fuckin woke me up. just do the interview and get the fuck out of here.

cousin : alright you are the boss.

cut to

mathew goes back to bed.

cut to

mathew wakes up. and he hears a tv sound.

mathew comes out and watches his cousin is still in the house.

mathew : didnt you have an interview.

cousin : yeah they called me, they said its tommorow.

mathew : that means you ar gonna stay one more night over here.

cousin : no i will just do the dinner and call it a night. come on we are going for dinner.

mathew : im not going anywhere. i havent had the break fast yet.

cousin : you have have the breakfast i'll do the dinner. come i told you its my birthday.

mathew : alright i know a place.

mathew takes him to the same burnt restaurant.

mathew goes inside eats food and the counter guy watches him in shock.

they both sit in the table and everyone rcognizes mathew and gets scared.

mathew orders a cake with candles to the counter with the unblowable candles. the counter guy gets scared.

mathew comes on the table and sits again.

cousin : lets have a drink. it will be fun .

mathew : no, i aint drinking.

cousin : please its my birthday, lets take some shots.

cousin yells "please send some flame shots"
all the waiter in the bar stares at them.
cousin and mathew sitting on the table.
the waiter comes with 2 flame shots
mathew : i havent drinked any flame shots before.
waiter : its ok, i can bring the normal drinks if you want.
mathew : na its his birthday.
they bothe drink the flame shots.
mathew drinks and says yuks and yells " we need some more flame
shots"
all the waiters and the owner watches them.
the owner : what the fuck is gonna happen now.
the waiter comes with a cake and starts .
cousin : ohhh a cake so thought full of you. this is going to be my
best birthday ever.
mathew : come on now, just blow the fuckin candles.
cousin blows the candle and the candle burns again
mathew laughs.
cousin : real funny.
mathew : come on give one more shot.
the ownerto the waiter : why did you give him unblowable candles.
waiter : he asked for it.
mathew : you got to wish first.
cousin : i wish that my cousin let me stay for a day more. [cousin
blows the canndle]
mathew lifts the cake : what you planned this all, make me drrunk
and let me stay one more day. its not gonna work asshole
mathew throws the cake and the cake hits the curtains on the wall
and annd the unblowable candle burns and the curatins lits on fire.
cut to
the entire hotel catches the fire. again the fire brigade shot.

cut to

mathew and cousin in the police station.

the police talking to the owner .

and mathew from the lock up . " sir, im a very decent guy, just put him inside, its his birthday. he made me drink forcefully.

cousin : just shhut the fuck up. you lit the hotel on fire.

the owner from the seat : twice

cousin : on my birthday what have i got my self into.

which ever police comes mathew "sir please let me go, its his birthday beat him. leave me "

all the police looking at cousin in anger.

mathew does this several times and cousin says it was a big mistake to come down to your house.

mathew again does the same.

cousin : just shut it will you.

there comes the officer : mental you again. i told you it was your last chance. you have left me no other option.

cut to

mathew in the mental hospital shots.

in queue with mad poeple for food.

mathew taking medicine.

everyone mad around him and mathew is silent.

cut to

few months later

cut to

mathew with the officer.

officer : i came to see you, im feeling bad for you. how are you doing here.

mathew : im doing great here. when i will be out.

officer : when you get cured.

mathew : show me that sun glasses. can i keep it.

officer : what you will do with it.
mathew : when i will go out, i will wear it in sun.
officer : i dont think you will be out soon. but take it.
mathew wearing it and likeing the glasses and looking here and there.
officer : have fun mental, i will come again soon.
the giards take thhe mental away.and officers leave.
cut to
the silent night in the hospital. shots and suddenly the alarm bells.
and everyone come out of their cages.
cut to
doctor to officer. " i dont know who planned this, but they escaped, it
was a work of a genius.
officer to his deputy : alright you take his statement, and even all the
guards. miss no one.
officer wears his sunglasses.
watching the officer doctor say's "sir one more thing, there was a
patient with the same glasses. he was kind of a boss of everyone.
ofiicer to himslef : fucking mental. [song starts mama says knock you
down]
cut to
mathew wearing the glass in the bus and driving and all the patiensts
in the back.
mathew dashing the cars and evetyone on the streets. and driving,
people running away from him.
driving zigzag on the street. drone shot of the bus
the end

Contents